This Is the Dreidel

Abby Levine

ILLUSTRATED BY **Paige Billin-Frye**

Albert Whitman & Company
Morton Grove, Illinois

For my sister, Emily. —A.L.

By Abby Levine and Paige Billin-Frye:
This Is the Pumpkin
This Is the Turkey

Also by Abby Levine:
You Push, I Ride • What Did Mommy Do Before You?
Too Much Mush! • Ollie Knows Everything
Gretchen Groundhog, It's Your Day!

Library of Congress Cataloging-in-Publication Data

Levine, Abby.
This Is the Dreidel / by Abby Levine;
illustrated by Paige Billin-Frye.
p. cm.
Summary: Max and his sister enjoy the dreidel and other special parts of
their family celebration. Includes nonfiction information on Hanukkah.
ISBN 0-8075-7884-3 (hardcover)
[1. Dreidel (Game)—Fiction. 2. Hanukkah—Fiction. 3. Stories in rhyme.]
I. Billin-Frye, Paige, ill. II. Title.
PZ8.3.L576Tf 2003
[E]—dc21 2003002606

The illustrations were done in colored pencil, acrylic, and gouache.
The typeface is Jimbo.
The design is by Mary-Ann Lupa.

For more information about Albert Whitman & Company,
visit our web site at www.albertwhitman.com

This is the dreidel Max takes from the drawer
where he had placed it one year before.

This is the menorah, down from the shelf.
Max gets the polish and shines it himself.

This is the rainbow of candles. Who'll choose one for the shammash, and others we'll use?

This is the sun sinking low. Time to start!

This is the blessing Max knows by heart,
over the candles his sister will choose—
reds and yellows and purples and blues—
in the menorah, down from the shelf,
golden and gleaming, Max polished himself,
after the dreidel comes out of the drawer
where Max had placed it just one year before.

These are the windows where candles are bright—

there's one for the shammash and one for each night.

These are the gifts we give one another,
mother and father, sister and brother.
Max decorated a tall picture frame.
Ruth drew the family and spelled out her name.

These are the relatives at the door!
This is what Max has been waiting for!

These are the latkes, piled on the plate.
Max is so hungry he says he'll eat eight!

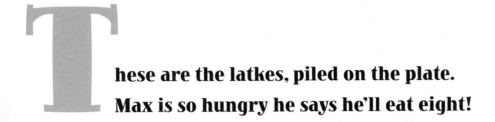

This is the dreidel Max spins on the floor.
He hopes that he doesn't get "Nun" anymore.

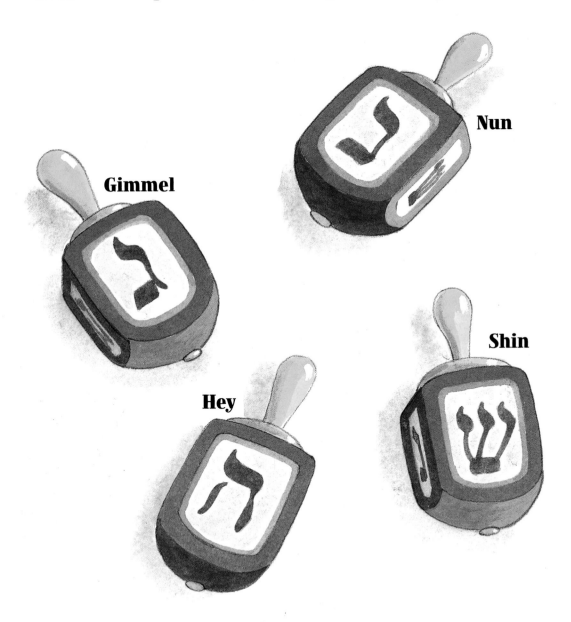

Nun

Gimmel

Shin

Hey

These are the stories we tell about:
the oil, and the flame that wouldn't go out;

Antiochus; Judah, the great Maccabee;
the Temple soiled; the Temple made free.

These are the songs that we sing to declare
that once "a great miracle happened there."

These are some presents of Hanukkah gelt;
better eat quickly—or else they will melt!

This is the pushke. And it's a good deed
for Max to give money for people in need.

This is the family, gathered around,
watching the candles, like stars, burning down,
after the stories and songs that declare
that once a great miracle happened there,
the latkes, the gelt, and the guests at the door,
all of the things that Max waited for;
the pushke that's filled, for it's a good deed
to help other people when they are in need,
the gifts that the family shared with each other,
brother and sister, father and mother.
Goodbye to the candles, so brave and so bright;
goodbye to the wonder of Hanukkah lights!

This is the dreidel Max puts in the drawer
till the eight days of Hanukkah come 'round once more.

Dreidel (DREY-duhl) A four-sided top used in a game played at Hanukkah. The Hebrew letters Nun, Gimmel, Hey, and Shin appear on the dreidel's sides. They stand for Nes Gadol Hayah Sham ("A Great Miracle Happened There"). To play the game of dreidel, children put nuts, raisins, or Hanukkah gelt into the "pot" and spin the top. If it lands on Nun, the player gets nothing. For Gimmel, the player takes the whole pot. For Hey, the player takes half. For Shin, he or she must put something in the pile.

 The dreidel game once had a more serious purpose. Under King Antiochus's rule, Jews would study and pray together in secret. If the Syrian soldiers discovered them, they would pretend to be playing a game with the tops.

Gelt (GELT; pronounced like "melt" with a hard "g") The Yiddish word for money. Gifts of Hanukkah gelt can be real coins or, often, chocolate "coins" wrapped in foil.

Hanukkah (HAH-noo-kah) More than two thousand years ago, King Antiochus IV of Syria ruled over the Jewish people. Because he followed Greek ways, he said all his subjects must do the same. On pain of death, the Jews were to stop practicing their religion. His soldiers destroyed the Temple of the Jews in Jerusalem and made it a Greek temple.

 A group of Jewish warriors called Maccabees fought the king's army and won back the Temple in 165 B.C.E. They restored the Temple, but when the priests looked for oil to rededicate the Temple and light the sacred lamp that was always kept lit, they could find only enough for a single day. Yet the oil lasted for eight days, until new oil could be made. Today Jews light Hanukkah candles for eight days to commemorate this miracle. (The word Hanukkah means "dedication.")

Latkes (LAT-kehz) Potato pancakes, fried in the oil that symbolizes the holiday.

Menorah (meh-NOR-ah) The Hanukkah menorah, or hanukkiah (hah-NOO-kee-yah), holds nine candles: one for each of the eight nights of the holiday, and a ninth one, the shammash (SHAH-mehsh) to light the others. Each night one more candle is lit until on the eighth night, all are aglow.

 The lamp that remained lit for eight days when the Temple in Jerusalem was rededicated is believed to have been a seven-branched menorah.

Pushke (PUSH-kee) A box to collect money for charity or tzedakah (tsah-DAH-kah). It is used in many Jewish homes.